To Brian and Jackie,
Remembering the fun times in Grandpa's basement.
-Mom

To Ripley,
Thanks for always being there.
- Michael

Published by
Copyright © 2022 by Barbara Renner
Illustrations Copyright © 2022 by Michael Hale

Library of Congress Control Number 2022916328
ISBN: 978-1-7357351-6-0 (Hard Cover)
ISBN: 978-1-7357351-5-3 (Soft Cover)

10 9 8 7 6 5 4 3 2 1
Design by Michael Hale
Printed in the U.S.A

Grandpa's

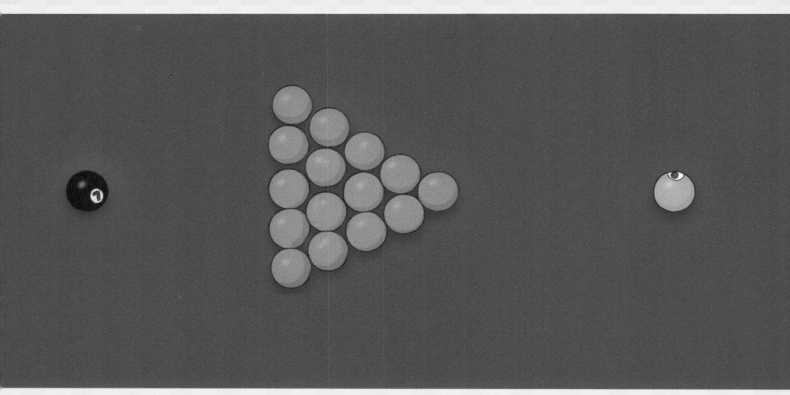

Written by Barbara Renner

Game Room

Illustrated by Michael Hale

Jack skips every other step as he races downstairs.

He remembers the cool basement air,
the tinkling piano sounds, and the dusty wood smell.

He's finally big enough
to play Grandpa's games.

He runs his fingers along the edge
of the big table and pokes
his hand into a corner pocket.

"Grandpa, let's shoot some pool."

They high five.

"Snooker has solid color balls.
I'll show you how to play."

Jack chooses a cue stick
and twists chalk on the tip.

Jack's eyes sparkle.
"That was fun. Your turn, Grandpa."

Grandpa places his hand on the table.

He bends forward.

He lines up his shot.

CLICK.

CRACK.

PLOP.

A red ball drops in the corner pocket.

"I wish I was good like you.
How did you learn to play snooker, Grandpa?"

"Professor Garibaldi
Hopsa Poppin Buttz
Green taught me..."

"Who? Is he real? You made him up."

Grandpa winks. They high five.

"Let's play again, Grandpa!"

Jack jabs too low on the cue ball.

It jumps over the edge and bounces on the floor.

A brass pot tips over.

Jack catches the ball before it bounces again.

"Sorry, Grandpa!" His cheeks burn.

"Good catch.
I think what we need is a little music."

Grandpa inserts a roll labeled *The Entertainer* in the player piano and flips a switch. The piano keys magically move up and down.

Music fills the air, and Jack snaps his fingers.

"Grandpa, I challenge you to a game of bowling."

"You're on!"

They high five.

It's Grandpa's turn. His hand covers the puck.
He eyes the lane. He pushes.

SWOOSH.
CHING CHONG... DING DING DING!

Numbers flip. Lights flash. A strike.

"You beat me again, Grandpa. How come you're so good at bowling?"

"Professor Garibaldi
Hopsa Poppin Buttz
Green taught me...
... and lots of practice."

"Are you sure
you didn't
make him up?"

Grandpa winks.

They high five.

"Let's play again, Grandpa."

Jack wraps his hand around the puck. He slides it back and forth. He hurls it toward the pins.

The puck speeds sideways to the edge of the machine.

It spins airborne...

... and breaks a lamp.

CRASH!

"Oh no, Grandpa, I'm sorry." Jack's shoulders droop.

"It looks like I'm lousy at bowling too.
I'll never be good at anything."

He slumps away.

The piano stops playing.

He adjusts the bench.

He cracks his knuckles.

He lines his fingers on the keys.

When Grandpa hears the musical chords, he turns to look.

"Jack, how did you learn to play the piano so well?"

"Maybe Professor Garibaldi Hopsa Poppin Buttz Green taught me...

... and I practice a lot."

Jack winks.

They high five.

A TRIBUTE TO JOHN ALLEN FARR
1912 - 1994
By Barbara Renner

The Grandpa in Grandpa's Game Room is based on my dad, John A. Farr. He was known for his sense of humor and was quite the adventurer. He and his buddies in Michigan belonged to the Polar Bear Club. Every year from November to April, they took the Polar Bear Challenge by swimming for 10 minutes once a week in the icy waters of Lake Huron.

After he moved to New Mexico, my dad found a new set of buddies who enjoyed playing a billiards game called Snooker on his Snooker table in the basement. In turn, he taught me, my brother, and later, his grandchildren, how to play.

Always ready to tease the grandchildren, Grandpa would pretend to pull off his thumb, hide surprises in an old cigar box, and talk about his imaginary friend, Professor Lucifer Garibaldi Hiapopus Transaviskia Herziagog Butts Green. I shortened the professor's name in the story so it would be easier to say while reading.

SNOOKER

Snooker is a billiards game that was created in 1875 by officers of the British Army stationed in Jubbulpore (Jabalpur), India. There are several differences between Snooker and Pool. Snooker tables are larger, but the pockets are smaller, and Snooker balls are smaller than Pool balls. British Snooker is played with fifteen solid red balls, six solid balls of different colors, and a white cue ball. American Snooker balls are the same colors as British balls, but the six different colored balls include numbers indicating their point worth.

What are some favorite stories about your Grandpa?